Grandpa Loves You!

For Al and Jean Ferris and their grandson EJ
—Helen Foster James

For Mum and Dad — thank you
— Petra Brown

Sleeping Bear Press™

2395 South Huron Parkway, Suite 200
Ann Arbor, MI 48104
www.sleepingbearpress.com

Printed and bound in the United States.

10 9 8 7 6 5 4 3 2 1

Library of Congress Cataloging-in-Publication Data

James, Helen Foster, 1951-
Grandpa loves you! / written by Helen Foster James;
illustrated by Petra Brown.
pages cm
Summary: A rabbit grandfather welcomes a new grandchild and looks
forward to spending time together and sharing many adventures.
ISBN 978-1-58536-940-9
[1. Stories in rhyme. 2. Grandfathers–Fiction. 3. Babies–Fiction.
4. Rabbits--Fiction.] I. Brown, Petra, illustrator. II. Title.
PZ8.3.J1477Gu 2016
[E]–dc23
2015027637

This book is presented to:

_____

On this day:

_____

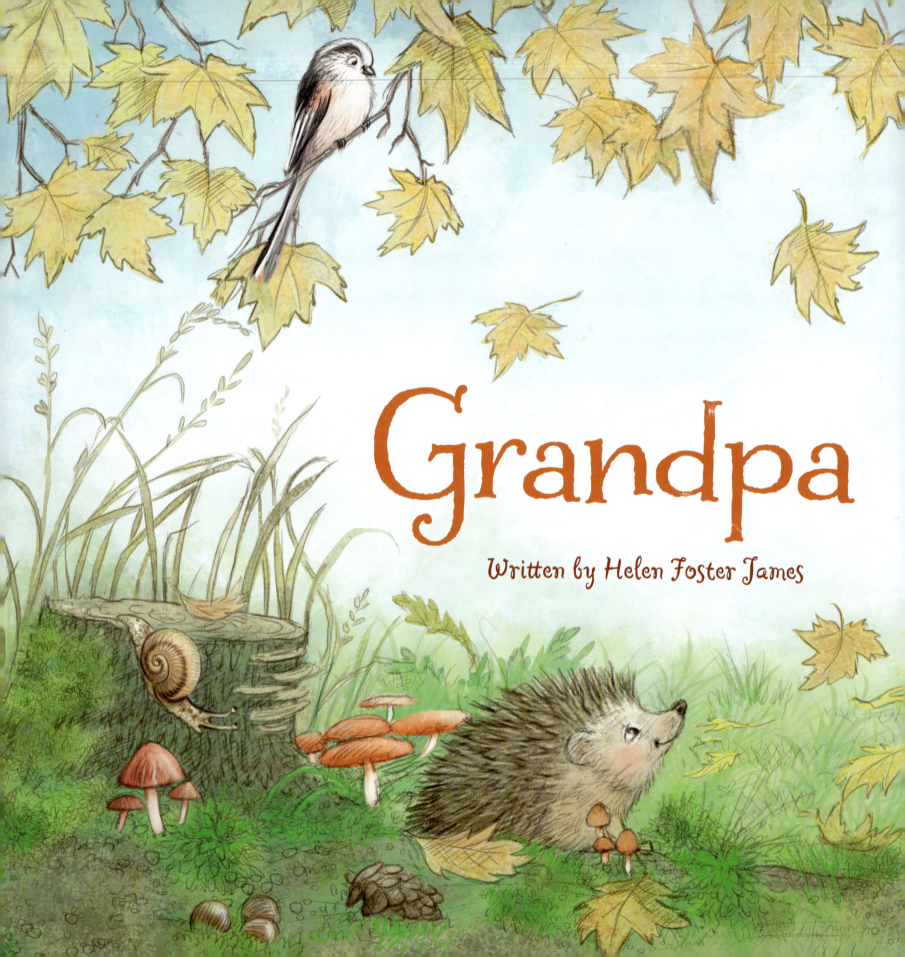

Grandpa

Written by Helen Foster James

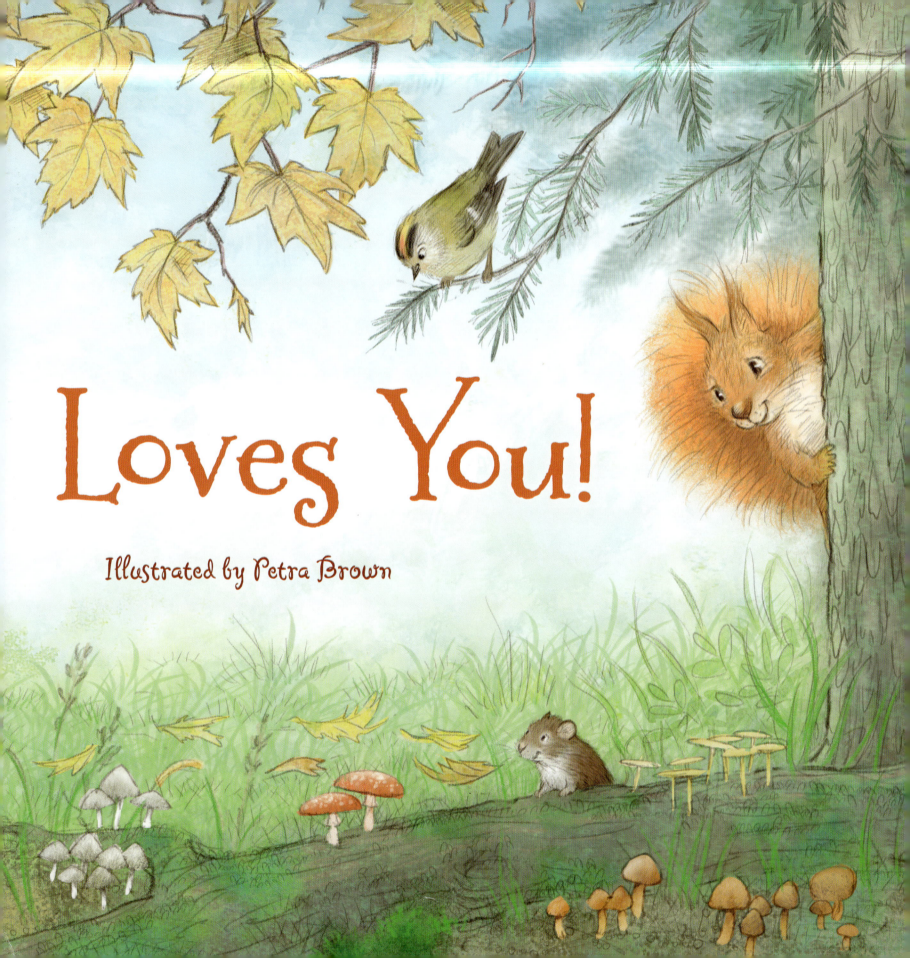

Loves You!

Illustrated by Petra Brown

The moment we met
I knew you would be

a fine little branch
on our family tree.

Life is much better
with you, little one,

cutie pah-tootie,
my bundle of fun.

I'll twirl you around
and swing you so high.

Hold on to grandpa
and reach for the sky.

Honey, grand bunny,
we'll hop and we'll hike.

We'll fly a new kite
and do what you like.

Side by side, pumpkin,
we'll tinker and fix.

I'll tell you my jokes
and teach you my tricks.

Be brave and take chances,
have fun and enjoy

each moment, my love,
my pride, and my joy.

When evening arrives
I'll wish you, "Good night."

I'll tuck you in bed
and whisper, "Sleep tight."

Sweetie pie, bunny,
adorable you,

my buddy, my pal,
I love you, I do!

A Special Letter to My Grandchild

_____

_____

_____

_____

_____

_____

_____

_____

With Love, _____

Paste a picture of grandpa
and grandchild here.